★ COUNTY FAIR ★

RAYMOND BIAL

Houghton Mifflin Company
Boston   1992

Acknowledgments

I would like to thank Mary Lee Donovan for her valued support and hard work in editing this book; the Champaign County Fair Association and Link Carnivals for their cooperation; and all the wonderful people at the fair who helped make this book possible, especially the carnival workers.

The photographs for this book were taken with Nikon N8008 and Canon AE1 cameras. Fujichrome slide film, notably Velvia, was used.

Library of Congress Cataloging-in-Publication Data

Bial, Raymond.
   County fair / Raymond Bial.
     p. cm.
   Includes bibliographical references.
   Summary: Text and photographs describe the happenings at a county fair.
   ISBN 0-395-57644-X
   1. Agricultural exhibitions—Juvenile literature. 2. Fairs—Juvenile literature. [1. Fairs. 2. Agricultural exhibitions.]
I. Title.
S552.5.B53   1992   91-23673
630'.74—dc20   CIP
                    AC

Printed in the United States of America

WOZ 10 9 8 7 6 5 4 3 2 1

For Linda, Anna, and Sarah

Throughout the year the fairgrounds stand quietly at the edge of town. Near the end of July, however, groundskeepers scatter bright straw in the livestock barns, spruce up the exhibit hall, grade the racetrack in front of the grandstand, and stake out the midway. A sense of anticipation begins to grow at the fairgrounds.

Loaded with the carnival rides, the first semitrailers arrive a few days before the fair opens.

Every year 125 million people attend one or more of the 3,200 local, county, and state fairs held in the United States. The word *fair* is actually derived from the Latin word *feria*, which means holiday.

Today, many people are drawn to fairs by the excitement of the midway and grandstand. Other people bring livestock to be judged or produce and canned goods to be displayed in the exhibit hall, because fairs are still very much rooted in agriculture.

As opening day approaches, farm trucks begin to pass through the gates to the livestock barns. Station wagons head for the exhibit hall. Over by the grandstand, brightly painted cars assemble on the track for the demolition derby to be featured on Friday, the first night of the fair.

By Friday afternoon, the quiet field and empty buildings have come fully to life with the sounds, sights, smells, and other sensations of the fair.

★ THE ★
LIVESTOCK
BARNS

The livestock barns are filled with the fragrance of alfalfa and clover hay. Cattle stand tethered with rope halters. Hogs flop down in their pens. Sheep don't seem to like the heat and the goats are always looking for a way to get out.

Exhibitors keep busy feeding, watering, and cleaning up after their stock. The boards of the stalls have been worn smooth over the years as generations of livestock and exhibitors have taken up residence during the week of the fair.

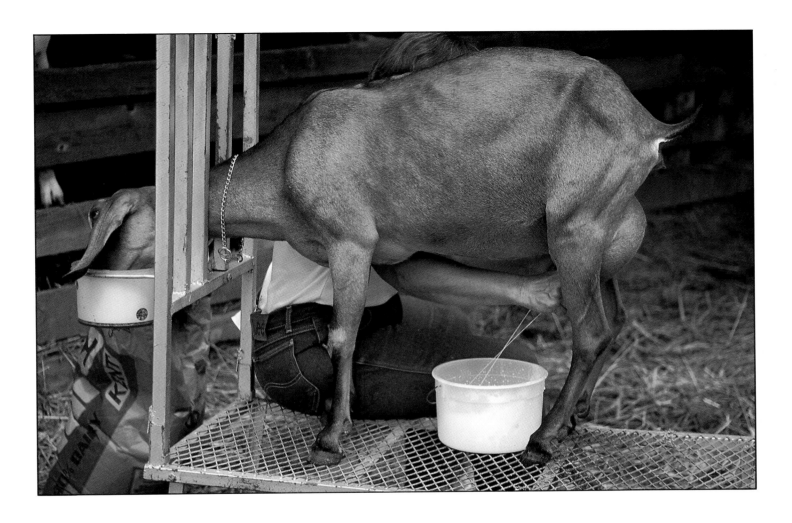

Held in Berkshire County, Massachusetts, in the early 1800s, the first American fairs were primarily livestock competitions. To this day, the judging of farm animals remains the most important activity at the fair.

A fair would be no more than a carnival without the livestock judging and the various competitions in the exhibit hall. Over the course of the week there will be open competitions, which anyone can enter, as well as junior and 4-H competitions.

Many young people participate in the livestock judging as members of 4-H or Future Farmers of America. These organizations help many of them to become better farmers, and all of them to become mature adults.

By caring for their stock, young people develop a strong sense of responsibility. They will often camp out on canvas cots alongside their animals while at the fair. They bring everything they need, from hair dryers to fresh clothes, in boxes and trunks.

The excitement begins with the judging. Many people have prepared their livestock all year just for this special day.

The judging begins early in the morning and continues until late in the afternoon for the entire week of the fair. The competition permits both young and old to demonstrate their skills in animal husbandry and to share knowledge about farming practices.

Over the years livestock has been significantly improved through these competitions, as farmers have striven to breed animals of the highest quality.

Exhibitors are awarded ribbons and prize money called premiums. Premiums have helped to attract a larger number of entries at fairs. Winning animals may be advanced to the state fair to compete for additional prizes.

Small animal competitions give people an opportunity to exhibit their finest purebreds. Often, urban youths who do not have room for two-thousand-pound steers in their backyards will raise small animals as a 4-H project. Judges carefully examine each entry to determine how closely it matches standards for the breed.

The week of judging ends with the goat show, which is always a popular event because these creatures have such charming personalities!

★ THE ★
EXHIBIT HALL

THIRD
PLACE

CHAMPAIGN
COUNTY
FAIR

FIRST

No.
03070
Exhibitor No. 6-06
Dept. K
Division
Sec.   Class 2453
Entry White Potatoes

Exhibitor Bette Bernius

No.
0479

Domestic arts have been highly valued at American fairs since the days when women preserved foods, sewed clothing, and made practically everything else that was needed in the home.

Fairgoers cannot help but be deeply impressed by the success of American agriculture, exemplified by the variety of products on display. These competitions have led directly to a higher standard of living for farm families and for everyone who likes to eat, dress, and generally live well.

Garden produce and field crops occupy a large portion of the exhibit hall. Tables are laden with onions, carrots, potatoes, and many other vegetables. On the walls, oats, barley, wheat, and tall stalks of corn are displayed. Apples and other fruits from the orchard line shelves on yet another wall.

As in the case of livestock judging, these competitions have helped farmers to substantially improve the quality of their crops and produce over the years.

Canned peaches, dill pickles, relishes, jellies, and jams are all proudly displayed at the fair.

When safe canning methods were developed around 1825, canned goods assumed greater importance as a way to store the bounty of the garden and the orchard in cellars and pantries.

Special cases are filled with pies, fancy cakes, breads, and other baked goods.

Quilts, baby blankets, handmade dresses, and other fine needlework grace the north end of the exhibit hall. Glossy green tables are crowded with floral arrangements of all sizes and types.

Collectively, thousands of hours of labor have gone into the exhibits. While the judging itself is closed to the public, how happy exhibitors feel when they return to find blue ribbons placed on their entries!

Class Champion Pie
No. 3034
Millie Bonnell
Sidney

Class Skirt + Matching B...
1st Mary's C...
2nd Alic...
3rd
4th

Class Ladies' Unlined S...
No. 2848
Mary's Clark
Carlson
...thaus

★ THE ★
GRANDSTAND

Entertainments have always been part of fairs, ever since the early Olympics in Greece and the medieval market fairs in Europe.

On opening night at this fair, the demolition derby will generate an abundance of smoke, noise, and fun-filled damage. The crowd roars as the announcer gives the signal and the old clunkers begin to bash into each other.

The cars do battle until just one is left, battered but still chugging along.

The next day, the harness racing begins in earnest as sleek horses whisk sulkies and satin-clad drivers around the track. Except for the flicking of hooves and the jingle of harnesses, this sport is known for its quiet grace.

Harness racing is popular at many county fairs across the country, with several heats or races scheduled every afternoon and evening. The horses compete for a generous purse of prize money.

At one time, all of American agriculture depended literally upon "horsepower." Horses were used in the fields and to haul crops to market, as well as for basic transportation.

To this day many grandstand events, such as the rodeo and horse show, still involve horses. The horse show is divided into separate categories for Western and English saddles. Contestants demonstrate not only their riding skills, but the breeding and care of their animals.

No county fair would be complete without a tractor pull. Just as tractors have replaced teams of oxen, draft horses, and mules for tasks requiring strength on the farm, so too have they replaced them in fair competitions. Now spectators watch tractors, not animals, pull sleds of weights as far as possible down the track. Winners receive cash prizes.

This competition includes the "Barnyard Special" for young farmers and the "Super Farmer" category for adults.

★ THE ★
MIDWAY

Everyone strains eagerly to take in all of the color, motion, and excitement of the midway. Fairgoers purchase tickets for rides and other entertainments, such as the haunted house and a maze of mirrors called The Puzzler.

The carnival on the midway did not really become an integral part of the fair until the Columbian Centennial Exposition in 1893. The exposition featured the world's first Ferris wheel, and the term *midway* is drawn from this event.

The rides have thrilling names, such as Tilt-a-Whirl, Round-up, Viking, Giant Swing, Enterprise, Scrambler, Raiders, and Sky Wheel. Of course, there are also the bumper cars, the roller coaster, and the merry-go-round, as well as a special section of rides for very young children.

On all of the rides, fairgoers may be assured of being flung, spun, bumped, and flipped in one or more directions, often at high speeds.

Most fairs are now geared for the family. Side show oddities such as bearded ladies and tattooed men have been eliminated.

Games are no longer rigged, but the odds still may not be to the customer's advantage. Even the most disciplined person can't resist taking a chance at a game, like darts or ring toss, at least once.

Stuffed animals hang from the inside walls of the game booths and, sitting on the counters, carnival workers beckon to everyone who passes by.

The midway also features tents of farm equipment, booths sponsored by political parties, a butterfly pork chop grill, the 4-H milkshake stand, and many other attractions.

Food concession stands, called "joints," offer treats ranging from corn dogs smeared with thick, yellow mustard to pink swirls of cotton candy. Everywhere, colorful signs encourage people to indulge in these tempting foods.

Lights flash on all the rides and music blares from loudspeakers. The air is filled with the greasy scent of corn dogs, elephant ears, and funnel cakes, as well as the faint perfume of lemon shakeups.

People line up at the rides, crowd around the games, purchase lots of snacks, and drift up and down the midway, trying to take in as many of the amusements as possible.

As the sun eases below the horizon, the midway is lit up against the darkening sky of the hot summer night.

Children grip their tickets in sweaty fingers. Shadows of the riders blur past. People try their hands at skeeball or allow a carnival worker to guess their ages and weights.

With the buzz of activity, it seems impossible to experience everything that is offered. Before long, there is time for just one more game, one more snack, and one last ride.

The week of the fair always goes by quickly.

As the final event, a country and western singer performs to cheers and wild applause in the grandstand. The rides, joints, and games on the midway close at midnight, and the carnival workers immediately begin to "tear down" the rides. Working all night and into the morning, they load the parts back onto the semitrailers.

Exhibitors load up their livestock and their produce, and head home again.

The next day, scattered litter is the only reminder that the fair was here. The livestock barns and exhibit hall are empty, except for the piles of straw bedding. The grandstand is quiet, as tractors equipped with rakes smooth over the hoof marks and tire tracks.

The fair will be back again next year. In the meantime, everyone takes home good memories of thrills on the midway and grandstand, a few souvenirs, and maybe even a blue ribbon or two.

Bibliography

The following books were consulted in the preparation of *County Fair*:

Marti, Donald B. *Historical Directory of American Agricultural Fairs*. New
    York: Greenwood Press, 1986.
Moss, Miriam. *Fairs and Circuses*. New York: The Bookwright Press, 1987.
Perl, Lila. *America Goes to the Fair: All About State and County Fairs*. New
    York: William Morrow, 1974.